purr
purr

MY
PET
HUMAN
Takes Center Stage

Also by Yasmine Surovec

MY PET HUMAN

PET HUMAN

Takes Center Stage

Yasmine Surovec

ROARING BROOK PRESS
New York

Published by Roaring Brook Press
Roaring Brook Press is a division of Holtzbrinck Publishing Holdings Limited Partnership
175 Fifth Avenue, New York, New York 10010

mackids.com

Library of Congress Control Number: 2016932245
ISBN: 978-1-62672-074-9

Our books may be purchased in bulk for promotional, educational, or business use.
Please contact your local bookseller or the Macmillan Corporate and Premium Sales Department
at (800) 221-7945 ext. 5442 or by e-mail at MacmillanSpecialMarkets@macmillan.com.

First edition 2017
Book design by Roberta Pressel
Printed in the United States of America by LSC Communications, Harrisonburg, Virginia

10 9 8 7 6 5 4 3 2 1

For Alex, Victor, Puppy,
and the cats

CONTENTS

CHAPTER 1
Oliver's First Day of School

My Name is Oliver. This is my pet human, Freckles. I have her well-trained. She feeds me treats. She rubs my belly. But today she's going to a new place of training. It's her first day of school.

I can't go? But I don't want to get stuck here at home all day. Sure there are some fun things at home: the empty boxes, the tuna and olive sandwiches. But the best part of home is Freckles.

Besides, I've been to Freckles's school once. It has a really big litter box. Humans call it a sandbox.

I try to change Freckles's mind. But today, all she can think about is school.

So I take matters into my own paws. She's not leaving without me. Not if I can help it.

While she's tying her shoes, I sneak inside her backpack. It's a tight fit, and her markers keep poking me from behind!

But it's no big deal. I need to make sure that Freckles will be okay. She's my pet human, after all.

We ride the bus to school . . .
We walk down the hallway . . .
Okay, time for me to get out. It's stuffy in here!
OOF!

Look at these kids crowd around.

Oh look! It's Liam. He's the pet human of my buddy George. He's also Freckles's friend.

Eep! The kids rub my belly. Tickle my cheeks. Squeeze my paws. I've never gotten so much attention!

But what about Freckles? I can see that she's frowning, and I can tell that she isn't too pleased about me being here.

Finally, I'm handed back to Freckles.

Then some guy with fur on his face comes over and interrupts.

CAN HE STAY?
I widen my eyes.
I blink.
WELL, HE CAN'T BE ROAMING AROUND.
They can't put me back in the backpack, either.
I KNOW! WE CAN TAKE HIM TO THE FUR-EVER FRIENDS CLUB.

Of all the names they could name their club, seriously, they chose "Fur-ever Friends?"

But do they serve olive and tuna sandwiches?

The Fur-ever Friends Club is in one of the classrooms. And inside, there's a lady. Something tells me she really likes cats.

Freckles asks if I can stay there until the end of the day. Or, you know, they could let me go home. Though I might stop by a few back alleys for some grub on the way. The Twirling Fork is the best.

Turns out, Fur-ever Friends isn't just for kids who like animals. The club does lots of good stuff too.

Next thing I know, Freckles is joining the club. So is Liam. And I have to wait while the cat lady goes on about the fund-raiser forever. I mean, fur-ever. And my tummy is grumbling.

Will someone rub my belly please?

Freckles and her friends find the idea of a fund-raiser exciting. The very thought of it makes me yawn.

A "cat and dog fashion show"? You can't make this stuff up.

ANOTHER KITTEN? In MY house?
Um, I don't think so!

It just wouldn't work. I need my space. I'm an "only-cat" kind of cat. I don't need a kitten in the house to keep.

No. Just . . . no. I don't want a kitten on my turf!

THAT'S MY HUMAN!
!

CHAPTER 2

An Annoying Guest

Saturday morning, Freckles's mom goes to the shelter. Ugh. I'm not looking forward to meeting the kitten.

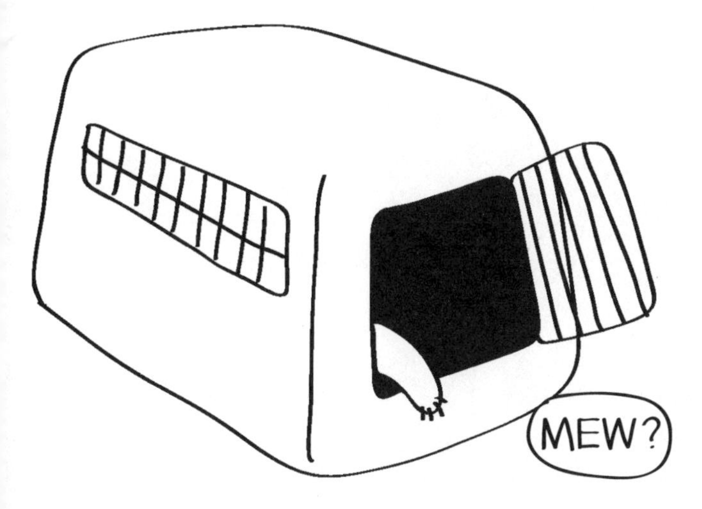

I'll bet she's going to be a gross and ugly kitten, and she's going to scare Freckles away.

See how annoying and hideous she is?

She's not shy at all.

She plays with
my favorite box.

She eats my kibble.

She's just arrived, and she already acts as if
she owns the place.

She's got my humans wrapped around her little paw.

She is NOT the cutest little thing. I'M the cutest little thing!

It seems like Freckles can't get enough of her, though.

The little kitten tries to snuggle up with me too. Yuck. I'd rather snuggle with a pineapple.

I'm outta here. I'm heading out to Ben's.

Ben the dog is my trusted friend. He has a human family with more kids than I can count on two paws.

My friends Farah and George are at Ben's house too. It's good to have friends to confide in.

Sometimes, humans just don't get it. But my friends do.

My friends are usually pretty good
about making me feel a little bit better.

And they sometimes have some pretty good advice.

Maybe he's right.

ANYWAY, I'M HEADING BACK. I JUST NEEDED TO GET AWAY FOR A BIT.

I go back home with a plan. Maybe if I perform my old tricks, they'll notice me.

I sing.

I juggle the toilet paper.

I play hide and seek.
SO CUTE AND FLUFFY!
HMPH!
But I'm still ignored.

A lot of things annoy me, but this takes the cake. Now they want me to be her friend.

Call me when she's gone. In the meantime, I'll be in my box.

Anyone, PLEASE make her stop.

But my humans think it's hilarious.

AGH! Not my precious treats!

I'm starting to get a headache. I'm going to take a nap.

PURR

CHAPTER 3

Freckles's Pet Project

It's been three days since the kitten came to live with us, and she's getting on my last nerve. I'm so glad Freckles is home from school.

THAT SOUNDS WONDERFUL.
HERE ARE SOME SNACKS FOR YOU GUYS.

Freckles and her friends start talking about the fund-raiser and pet fair. Yawn.

I'M THINKING OF CREATING A RAT OBSTACLE COURSE WITH MY DAD. GEORGE SEEMED TO ENJOY IT LAST TIME WE MADE ONE.

THAT SOUNDS AWESOME, LIAM. I'M THINKING OF DOING A FASHION SHOW. IT'LL BE THE CUTEST THING EVER!
GRR

AND NOW WE HAVE PRINCESS PICKLES STRUTTING HER STUFF ON THE RUNWAY IN HER PINK TUTU AND HER DIAMOND-STUDDED TIARA!
EEE!
Note to self: Steer clear of Jin.

Both Liam and Jin know what they're doing for the pet show. Freckles is still stuck.

I COULD ALSO MAKE A CAT CASTLE OUT OF CARDBOARD BOXES.
OR NOT.

You've got to be kidding me. What does she mean by "train Oliver"? I train her. Not the other way around.

I remember that time. I couldn't figure out what she wanted, so I laid on the floor and took a nap.

THAT'S A GREAT IDEA IF YOU COULD MAKE IT WORK. I'VE NEVER BEEN ABLE TO TRAIN MY CAT.
OLIVER IS PRETTY SMART. I BET HE COULD LEARN TRICKS EASILY!
Correction: VERY smart.

Is she for real? I'm not going to take commands from anyone! And not in public!

After Jin and Liam leave, Freckles wants to get working right away.

Oh, goodie. I think I'm going to like this project. Cardboard boxes are involved. My favorite!

YOU'RE A SMART LI'L KITTEN. YES, YOU ARE! I'M GOING TO MAKE YOU A PART OF THE SHOW TOO.
How is SHE smart?!
All she does is roll around and purr! Every cat does that.
ROLL OVER, GIRL!
!

That's it, I'm going to put on an amazing performance at the show. Yup, you heard that right. I've decided that I'm going be a part of Freckles's show. She's MY human, after all, and I want her to succeed.

That, and whatever it takes to get her attention away from that little thing. I want my Freckles all to myself . . .

I'm looking at you, kitten.

SIT!
GOOD KITTIES!
HAVE A TREAT!

ROLL OVER!
GOOD KITTIES!

The best part of the training is the treats. And I get to show off how awesome I am.

All these tricks are so easy. I'm going to ace them all at the show.

YOU DID IT, KITTEN! FOLLOW HER LEAD, OLIVER!

Mmm, mmm, treats! Tuna bits, chicken munchies, li'l shrimps, and of course, olives! I love them all.

Is she kidding?

IS IT TOO LATE TO BACK OUT NOW?

CHAPTER 4

Cat-astrophe at the Fair

Quite a crowd came to the fair. I didn't think anyone would come. I mean, who would want to see a pet fashion show? Or a rat obstacle course? Or a couple of cats doing tricks?

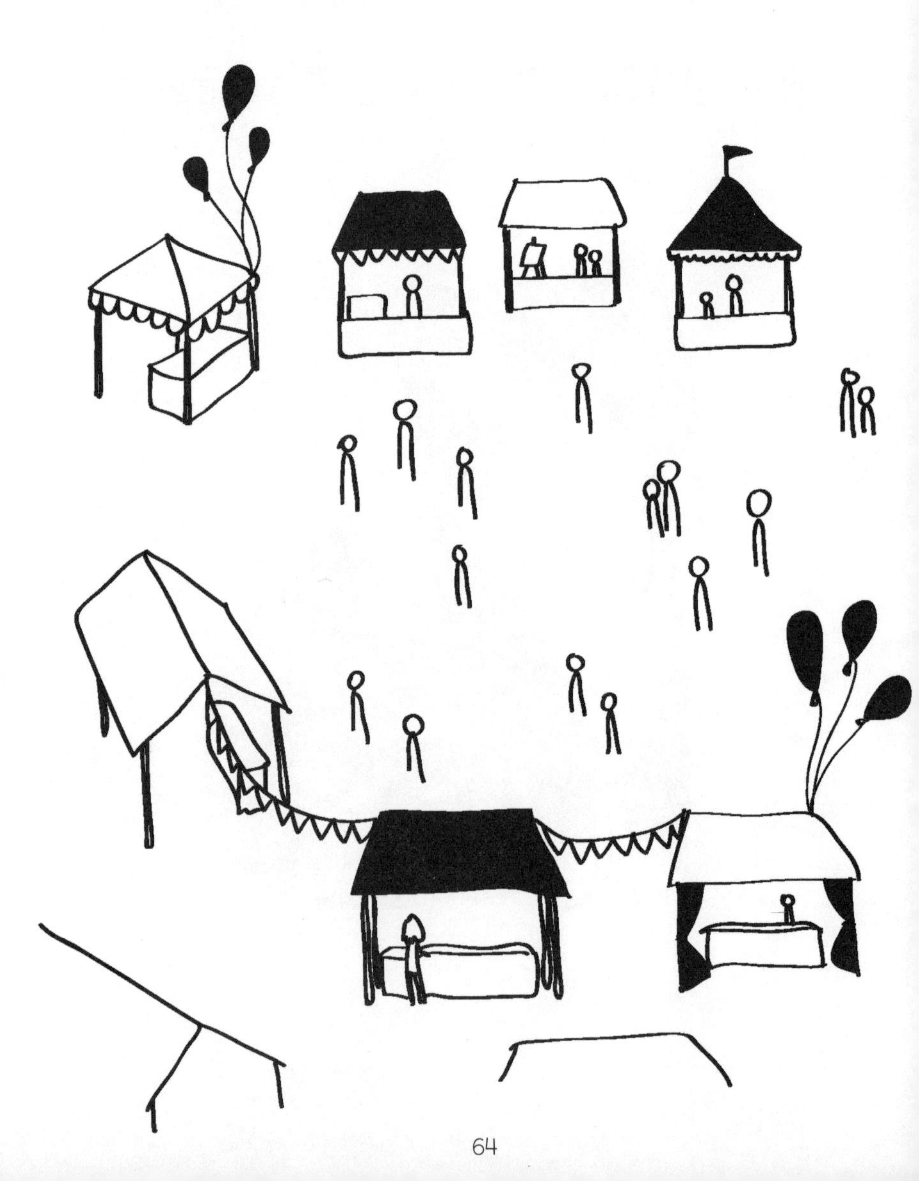

George has it easy. All he has to do is pass through a series of tubes to get to a piece of cheese.

Jin's cats and dogs, on the other hand, have to wear costumes. I'm glad I'm not in her fashion show.

I can tell that Freckles is jittery and nervous. Now I feel bad. I'll try my best to make our show a success. At least I don't have to wear a silly ball gown like Jin's cat.

Yikes! I think we're going to go on stage after Jin.

The show seems to be going well.

But Freckles gets even more nervous as she watches Jin.

Finally, we're on stage. Whoa! The crowd looks bigger from up here.

The crowd bursts out laughing.

Freckles is great. Like a pro.

But I feel like I can't see with the lights shining on me. I blink. A thought hits me. What if I don't do well? What if I mess up? I don't want to embarrass Freckles!

Ugh, my stomach.

The crowd is snickering. Freckles looks nervous, but she keeps going.

Oh no! The crowd breaks into full-on laughter.

OLIVER, WHY AREN'T YOU DOING THE TRICKS WE PRACTICED?
HA HA HA!
UH-OH. OLIVER'S NOT LOOKING TOO GOOD UP THERE.
HA HA HA!
HA HA HA!

I just want the show to end.
AND, UH, WHAT A GREAT COMEDIC ACT. JUST GOES TO SHOW, YOU CAN'T TRAIN A CAT!
OLIVER, ARE YOU OKAY, BUDDY?

And there went all the treats. Eating a lot and being nervous in front of a big crowd is not the best combination.

GRUMBLE!

CHAPTER 5
Fur-ever Friends

ADOPTIONS
YUP, THIS KITTEN IS AVAILABLE, AND SHE'S AN ABSOLUTE SWEETHEART.

Freckles has a vet check me out.

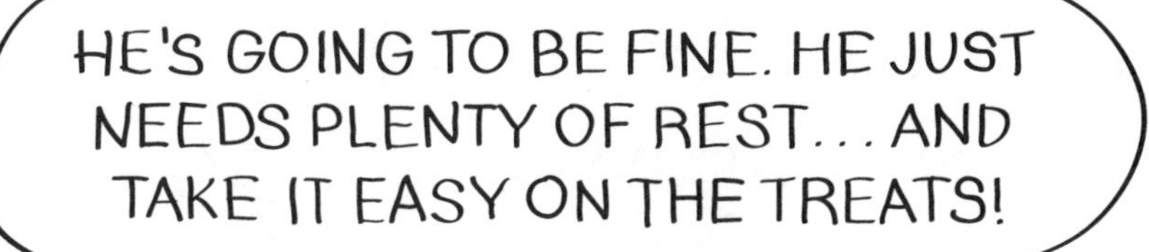

My tummy feels better, but now something else hurts. My heart (and my pride). I ruined the show for Freckles.

The Fur-ever Friends Club members gather by the booth to hear the results of the fair.

THIS IS MRS. ROY, AND SHE'S FROM THE SHELTER. SHE'D LIKE TO SAY A FEW WORDS TO EVERYONE INVOLVED.

THANK YOU SO MUCH! IT'S SO GREAT TO SEE KIDS ACTIVE IN THE COMMUNITY. THE PROCEEDS OF THIS FAIR WILL GO A LONG WAY IN EXPANDING OUR SHELTER. AND EVERYONE'S WELCOME TO VISIT US WHEN IT'S DONE!

AND THANKS TO JIN AND HER FASHION SHOW, SOME PEOPLE HAVE EXPRESSED INTEREST IN ADOPTING SOME OF THE CATS AND DOGS FEATURED!

MY MOM HELPED ME SEW ALL THE COSTUMES!

I'm so embarrassed, I feel like hiding. Mrs. Roy doesn't mention anything about Freckles's cat training show. Good thing my friends came around to make me feel a bit better.

Freckles is stressing out too. But she did a great job. I'm the one who couldn't handle myself on stage.

Believe it or not, Jin and Liam say we stole the show. Everyone thought we were so funny. It was the perfect way to end the night. I didn't ruin the show, after all!

And because the little kitten held her own under the lights, people kept asking about her at the adoption center.

I guess that's good news. Actually, I don't know.

I mean, I'll have my toys back.

And my boxes.

And my food.
THAT'S MY FOOD!
NOM!
OLIVER
And my bed.
THIS IS MY BED!
PURR
That's all good, right?

She has been entertaining,
at the very least.
I WONDER WHERE SHE COULD BE.
I'll miss playing hide and seek.
SQUIRM
I'll miss piling laundry on top of her.
PURR
PURR
I'll miss the belly rubs.

I wonder who's going to adopt her?

I got a bit teary-eyed seeing the kitten with Ben's family. I'm kinda relieved that she's gonna live close by. But don't tell anyone.

If there's a family who would love and pamper that kitten, it's gonna be Ben's humans.

But it sure is nice to have my
Freckles all to myself again.

BUT DON'T WORRY. I'VE GOT A BUNCH OF BELLY RUBS FOR YOU WHEN WE GET HOME.

FIN
WELL THAT LOOKS LIKE FUN.

The End

YASMINE SUROVEC

is the artist behind the blog Cat vs. Human. Originally from the Philippines, she now divides her time between California and Arizona with her husband, son, dog, and three cats.

purr
purr
purr
purr